I take you through the city, where it's picturesque and   at
u expect Scotland to look like. Well that's the tourist b

I take you to the underbelly where this story begins.

e go through an area where it's dark and depressing even on a sunny day, with granite houses
here the 60s and 70s idea of modern day living never worked. This is the type of area where bad
emories get made of, with stories you never hear in the paper cause it gets covered up for the
urist industry.

ith boarded up flats and shops like you've seen all over the years, with graffiti on the bus stops
at tell of what area it is. With waste land, burnt out cars and groups of ned's hanging outside the
ops like a moth to a lightbulb. Come and join me over the bridge and I'll tell you a story.

t me take you to the early 2000s where it all begins.

apter 1: Sunny Saturday

turday morning, Shane was in his kitchen having a pint of milk, when he heard a knock at the door.
was his mate Dave with a skateboard in his hand.

write man, ye coming oot?"

ye"

ey went oot, and walked down the close, where in front of the flat door, wis a group of bams.
ams, Neds, if yer older generation, schemies. What a mean by bams is they're all dressed in
acksuits with their socks up at their ankles, with their caps in the air, ye know what I mean.
yway, they hassled them.

way and pull yer troosers up, yeh fuckin sweaties eh?"

know, wee man syndrome, the mouthpiece eh the group.

ave turned around.

ye yer ma,"

What the fuck ye say about my ma?" says the wee bam, an got held back by his mate.

hat's Cocos little brother, don't go near him."

write Dave," says the guy who was holding him back,

write" Dave was brought up roond here, an' his brother had a bit of a reputation. Nobody would
art on Dave eh.

Anyway, we carried on, and started tryna skateboard. When we say tryna skateboard, we were'ny awf'y good, but thought we were quite decent cause we could pull an olly an' thought we were Tom Hawk. Dave was still raging about them fuckin bams.

"Fuckin', see if he fuckin says that to me again, I'll just rack ma nut on him." Dave had rage about it even if he wasn'y like 'em he still wasn't gonna take any shit.

You know, they dressed in baggies yeah, fuckin skateboard gear. Listened to a different sorta music they weren'y listenin to rap an' dance. Shane and Dave listened to fuckin metal. Problem is, bein a bit different, ye stand oot round here.

"Honestly Dave, just leave it eh?"

Anyway, they were skating away thinking of what tae do with our summer.

Shane said, "We should make a skating video. I could edit it, would be brilliant!"

Dave's like, "Aye, but we dinne have a video camera?"

"Aye, but your dad does eh?"

"I could ask him if we could 'ave a lend eh it for the day, or through the summer. You know, skating we do jackass, do some stunts, would be brilliant, would be a right fuckin laugh. Maybe send it to skate shops, see if it goes anywhere." said Dave.

Dave was still not letting' it go, bout that fuckin guys outside the flats. Shane said, "They're just fuckin schemies eh?"

"That's rich; we're from the schemes,"

"But we dinny act like that, fuckin' fuds."

That day, they kept on skating thinking of what they were gonna do that summer, grand plans of what video they were gonna make. Problem is, summer came and Shane had to go up north to visit his grannie, and then was away for 6 weeks. In those 6 weeks, everything changed.

When he came back, he met Dave in the stairs. He had to turn twice to look, was fuckin Dave.

"Awright Dave?"

"Awright"

"Fuck are ye dressed like a schemie for man?" he was there in a full tracksuit, wi a burberry cap sticking up in the air.

Dave was like, "you enjoyed yer holidays, away for the whole summer, I thought we were gonna make a skating video"

Shane said, "Never meant to be as long as I did, you know, ma mum sent me up there an aw. But I'm back doon now."

'Aw well, started hinging around with some other boys like." He was given a bit of a cold shoulder to Shane. You know.

'Aw you started hinging around wi all the bams eh, on the street"

He goes, "Naw they're sound. Difference is, lassies dinnae like sweaty looking, grungy looking guys man eh. You know what always happens, we always get started on by the stuff we wear eh" said Dave.

"So what. Now, now you a fuckin wee little fuckin ned aye?"

"Who the fuck you calling a fuckin ned?" said Dave, "you know what, jus fuck off eh"

Dave changed in the space of 6 weeks. Couldn't be bothered with Shane no more. Shane headed up in the lift where Dave left.

Shane sat in his room, where his room was covered in posters of slipknot, corn, even limp biskit. Sitting there watching the wrestling, Shane wasny bored. You know, Dave was a mate but times were changing. And he was quite happy being a loner. It was time for him stick to what he likes doing, bit of drama and art.

Few weeks went past then his phone rang, Shane answered it and it was Dave.

"Awrite man, whit ye up to the night?"

"Nout much."

"Fancy coming oot?"

"That'd be awrite, you know" Shanes thinks why not, thing is he'd been stuck in the house for a good few weeks daein nothing. Anyways a knock at the door, it was Dave wi all his new mates, the bams that they seen down at the bottom eh the flats.

"Awrite pal" said Dave.

Still seemed like he had a bit of attitude, seemed a bit wide eh. When I say wide, I mean cheeky. Anyway, Shane was a bit on edge going out, but went out anyway.

They were sitting in the park having a drink, a bevvy. Shane seemed like he was getting the brunt of all the cheek from everybody. Anytime he tried to stand up for himself he always had a bit of a wide answer straight away eh. You know it's only banter, it's only a laugh, but he seemed to get the brunt of it.

Shane sat quite quiet just trying fit in, where Dave was sort of picking on him. After a while they seemed to do this play fight. When I say play fight I mean it was a bit rough, everything below the neck was fine to hit as hard as you can. Was getting dead arms, and getting jelly babied where you get kneed in the legs. Again, Shane just though this was a way of them having fun, even if it was just him getting hit the whole time eh. Shane tried to fight back and have a laugh. Aye it was stiff and sore, but they're only mucking aboot.

Dave said, "Go an' fight, go an fight Ryan," Ryan looked like more o' the weaker bunch, where if it wisny for Shane being there, he would be the one getting picked on. Shane didny wanna do it, but it was only just mucking aboot. They started off wrestling; throwing digs here n there. Like a say, everything below the neck was fine, was still only toy fighting. Shane was getting the better o' Ryan then all of a sudden, a boot, right to the ribs and a knee, right in the fuckin arse. Shane was on the ground, where they all started stomping and kicking him. The whole group, stomping on his face and giving him punches in the mooth. This turned more rougher than mucking aboot. Shane still thought they were only having a carry on.

Adrenaline was rushing through Shane's body, he was starting to shake. This seems more serious now eh. The group stopped and walked away, Shane was on the ground trying to stand up, shaking off the mud from his top. Shane said nothing and just walked away. They were all shouting, "Aw we were only having a laugh! Dinnae be a pap, we were only carryin on"

Shane had enough, walked home and thought about it. *Was it a carry on?* Shane stupidly went back the next day, same nonsense happened for weeks, weeks and weeks. Shane had it in his mind, *it's just rough playing.*

His room started to change; he started takin down his posters. Even the way he started dressing was changing. He stopped wearing baggy clothes; he stopped wearing heavy metal t-shirts, started wearing trackies and labels. He had his friends at school, what was into what he was in to, if that makes sense. You know, they're still skater boys and goths. But he never seemed a part of that group any more; they seemed to change on him as well. Just the way he dressed.

Shane's attitude started to change slightly even the way he spoke a wee bit. He never fitted in there, and wisnae accepted by the guys in his area either. If Shane had any sense, he would have stayed away from them, but for some stupid reason he was so desperate to have friends, he stuck with them. Even if he was the brunt of the joke and he was the punch bag of the group. It wisnae because Shane was soft, think it was he had more of a nicer nature, and he kept on kidding himself, *this is a carry on*. Even all the cheek he got, made him feel like shit. It went over his head, thought was just the banter, just a laugh, just the way they played, if that makes sense.

Shane was getting off the bus after school, where he was walking to his flats. He opened the door and the lift was out of service. He was walking up the stair, where he meets Dave.

"Awrite man," Says Dave, "Fuckin hell, yer in the full gear now aren't ye eh?"

Shane was dressed in a full tracksuit and a cap. "How, what's wrong with this?" said Shane. "Aw nothing's wrong with it, jus you always said only neds wear fuckin tracksuits. How, think you're a ned now, ya wee wannabe?"

"Naw, just changing ma style"

"Aw well, ye coming out tonight?"

"Aye I'll be out"

"Aye we'll be all sitting in the close at 6 o'clock, just come roond" bothered him in the back of this mind, what Dave said. Calling him a wee wannabe, a wee wanna be ned. Shane used to slag neds the whole time, saying he would never be like that, an what's he doing, he's changing into that. He's still the brunt of the joke and still feels like a joke.

Shane left going out that night, instead he was sat in his hoose and played PlayStation, to just head to school the next morning.

Shane was at school, he felt isolated. There were no groups for him that he was hanging about with, the group he did hang aboot with, well, they left. He just sat on the stairs in the corridor where a guy John from his class came over. John was dressed in a black and white Fred Perry top wi a beanie hat, Burberry beanie hat.

"Awrite man, what ye doin sittin by yerself? A see you most days just floating aboot"

"Nah it's just..." Shane never knew what to say to them eh. Didn't wanna say he's got no mates, makes him seem like a right saddo eh. John seemed sound.

"Aye, see at lunch time just come round the back eh the bike sheds, that's where we all hang aboot"

So at lunch time Shane went round the back eh the bike sheds, where they were all smoking. Shane never smoked, but was awrite with it, more fags for them. They never ripped on Shane at all, they were actually quite sound to the whole group. So at lunch time they left the school and went out. John was telling the boys where Shane was from.

"Vit, yer fi Hillburn? Aw man, yer gonna fuckin chore our socks."

Shane explained himself, he goes "I'm no fae Hillburn, I stay there now but I'm fae up north"

"That's how you got the funny accent" They quite liked it. Made Shane feel welcome, made him already feel like a part eh the group. As he walked to the shops, there was a queue of school kids standing outside it. But they never queued, they just walked in and nobody said anything. Shane was drinking a bottle of coke when they walked out.

John says, "Can I have it"

Shane passed it to him where he launched it at a group of goths. John's group all pissed themselves laughing, goths did nothing. As they walked down the street, where it was just all devilment and a big carry on. Noising up shopkeepers by going in and pushing stuff over. Shane did it first in the laundrette, pushed a whole box of powder over and ran oot. It was a laugh; it was a carry on, like I said it was only devilment.

One of John's friends pointed over the wall and said, "Look it's a fuckin group of fuckin sweaties, let get em"

Not a moment too soon the boy jumped over the wall like he was fuckin in the grand national. Everyone leaped over the wall and started chasing this group. I mean it was like a big game of chase me, chase me where the slowest goth got caught and they all started booting fuck out of them. Shane kind of thought it's still a bit of a carry on, they weren't takin liberties. When he walked away, he was thinking *I turned into a person I don't like.* Trying to justify it by thinking it was just rough play.

Shane was sitting at the bus stop after school, where he was looking at the window going past all th areas. It's like a safari tour going round the different areas, how grim and depressing all these place are. And how some flats just look like they got a reputation and a notorious vibe just looking at them. For flat roof pubs and boarded up old flats and houses. Areas you won't see anywhere up th town. This is all on the outskirts of the city.

Chapter 2: A knock at the door

Shane was finished with his tea, sitting on the couch. Where at 6 o'clock bang, bang, bang, at the door. Shanes mum answered it; it was Dave and all his mates. Shanes mum looked at this group, looked at Dave. She hasn't seen Dave in a while. Shanes mum wasny one for judging eh, but they a looked jailbait. She probably wasny wantin Shane to be hanging aboot with them.

"Shane" said Shane's mum, Shane came through. She looked worried that Shane was going oot wit them.

Sitting in the stair in the close, where Ryan was burning 'mentions' with his lighter YLL and putting everyone's name on the wall, like that's a fuckin good idea. He started speaking about stories, biggin' themselves up, telling stories that he witnessed and seen. Was it true? Was it hammed up? Who knows? Shane was just thinking, he never seen any of this stuff in the paper. The same way it all could be true. Smelly Dale, in fact before Shane saw smelly dale nobody called him that to his face. Smelly Dale was telling a story about when he seen Danny boy, Danny Burns, got shot outside the chippy in the leg. Shane vaguely minds hearing about it.

Sam goes, "aye but I saw 2 junkies fighting outside the street then one of them went and chibbed him eh,"

Shane goes, "what did you do when you saw that"

"Fuckin just legged it, fuck that man"

You know, they're all actin hard with their stories and Shane was just hoovering it in, listening to it all. It was entertaining for a boring night sitting in the close.

All of a sudden they heard a bang, where it echoed down the stair. It was a neighbour that has had enough of them, running down the stairs, where they legged it. He was behind them, you could hea the footsteps echoing getting louder and louder. They opened the door and hid round the side of th lift, where the neighbour chased Dale and Ryan doon the stair. Shane and Dave pressed the button door to open the lift where they sneaked out the back of the flats and met Dale, Ryan an Sam.

"Fuckin hell man, that was close. Guy's a fuckin nutter."

Shane's pants were touching cloth, he nearly shit himself eh. They called it a night and he sneaked i where his mum still looked worried.

Vhere you been?" asks Shane.

ane said, "Just hanging aboot"

low do you smell eh weed?" Shane never smoked, they were but he wasny gonna say.

dunno it's no weed" Shane said, "I must be sitting too close to smelly Dale."

ane's mum never said anything.

eekend came and again, a knock at the door. They're all there. As they headed out, they thought day they would take a bus for something to do. A bus trip, here we go. They jumped on the 32 bus, hat is like a safari park tour for all of the shithole areas in the city. This is gonna be a laugh.

ey got off in Glenburn, where it was rough as fuck. Dale was writing mentions on the wall, writing LL". Where this young skinny looking boy, what looks like a junkie. only looked about 12. Wasny ally a junky, but you know what I mean, he looked drawn.

e seen them, "who are you?" he shouted over at 'em.

here Ryan, acting like the tinman, went and said, "We're from Hillburn ya bass"

ne boy cycled off quickly and whistled.

Vhy the fuck did ye say that Ryan?"

w fuck um eh. He's a wee boy hinking he was fuckin hard eh"

'a know he's gonna get his mates now eh?"

w what, a wee fuckin mini mob, whatever eh" Not a moment too soon, boys started appearing utside the stair, shouting,

'ou fi Hillburn? Fuckin, you're in the wrong area now" He started sprinting over at the, and they ok off. It was like a game of chase. Shane ran that fast he ran past Ryan, where he looked roond. van looked like he was ready to cry, shitting himself eh. They ran into a stair, they just made it and ot the door closed. They were banging on the door; they ran outside the back stair. Running rough the side, Shane could see them coming through the alleyway, just at the side of him. He ought I'm *never gonna make it*. The bus was up ahead. Dave and all that jumped on the bus, nane thought *they're gonna leave me behind, the bus is gonna take off.* Shane could hear them at e back of him, shouting and screaming. *They were gonna kick the fuck out me eh if I dinnae get on is bus.* Ryan shouted, "Come on, get on! The bus is isny gonna wait forever!"

unning that fast Shane thought his legs are gonna give way, as if the front of his body was going rward past his feet and he was just gonna fall at any moment. He got on the bus before the doors osed and it took off. He had change in his pocket but eventually found his day saver.

ney were laughing at the back eh the bus as it went roond the corner. He was so close to getting attered. His heart was pounding but it was good fun.

Chapter 3: Back to School

Hanging out at the playground with John and his mates; John goes, "Ye hear what happened to Malky?"

"Who's Malky?"

"Malky in S4; he wasny In the same class as us."

"Nah what happened to him?"

"Here he comes now. Here's Malky!" he shouted Malky over, "Ah what happened to you the weekend?"

Malky showed, he never even explained it, just pulled down his fuckin jeans an showed a scar where it's been stitched. "What happened to you like?" said Shane.

"Coz I got smashed at the weekend" The side of his right leg.

"What happened?"

He goes, "I was just walking home, and some guy just... I never even knew it, till I just felt a nip"

"Just a nip, fucking hell, looks like an absolute battle wound!"

"Never even realised it until I felt the warmth going doon my leg and realised he slashed me on the side of the leg"

"What? for no reason?"

He goes, "Aye, for no reason"

Dunno if that was Malky telling the whole story but, still. Shane thought his story getting chased through Glenburn on the weekend never seemed as mental as that.

Anyway school was finished and Shane was back home. Ryan was in his shed digging out shovels.

"Bingo!" said Ryan.

Shane goes "What're we getting shovels for?"

"Aw, we're getting shovels to dig a hole obviously, that's what you use shovels for" said Ryan, smar They all went along. Why are they digging a hole? It was that boring of a day ye need to dig a hole. They went on the wasteland with the flats surrounding. They went up to the top of a hill, and starte digging; Shane, Ryan, Dave and Tam. Right now, I haven't even mentioned Tam in this story. He wa a quiet guy; it's the quiet ones you gotta look out for.

They were digging away at the top of this hill, thinking they were doing a heavy graft for the day. Ryan's plan was, *we dig a hole and this is where we were gonna hang out.* It's no gonna be in the stair anymore, they were gonna just lie in a hole. Shane never got it, but he kept on digging anyway *It's gonna be like our trench, our hidey hole,* that was Ryan's great plan. To be fair, at night, you would never think there were 4 guys in the waste land. The hole was that deep enough that when you looked over you couldn't see them till they sparked up a fag, and you can see an orange glow in the distance.

The weekend came, and they went to the park. They were all sitting in the park dressed to impress with their Stone Island top and Helly Hanson jackets and Fred Perry tops, stinking of aftershave. Come too close with a fag and they'd probably go up in flames. The lassies came to meet them. Chelsea, Shantelle and Sarah-Jane and a couple of other group of boys, but, I'm no gonna mention them coz they're no really relevant to the story. Just everyone met up at the park. We all chipped in for a bevvy, Dave asked, "What does everybody want?"

Bottles of Bucky, Mad Dog and a bottle of voddy went roond, "Dale, what you wanting?" probably shocked, he said "sweeties"

"Naw ya dafty, what do you want, what you wanting to drink?" he was like " aw just a tenants"

We all chipped in and as Shane looked the oldest he was told "right you go to the shops"

Dave said to Shane "You're gonna get your hole the night"

If ye listen to Dave, Dave's shagged all the lassies eh. He started telling Shane a story he was with Shantelle when his mum was oot. He goes "aw I was shagging her in the room, shagged her that much the fuckin neighbours complained about the smell like eh". Anyway that was Dave's version of the story. They heard later he couldn't get it up, he got fanny fright.

Anyway, the rest eh the boys go "aye fuckin get wi Sarah Jane eh. Fuckin she seems a bit tight. But a bet if you get drink, and get a couple of drinks in her, ye probably could finger her eh?" said Ryan. Shane was just takin this in; he was too shy to even say much at this point to the lassies.

He went with a lass to the shops. Dale had handed him a motor bike helmet to hold in his hand, "Aye they're gonna think yer older eh, coz yer driving a bike. Baba's no gonna give a fuck, just as long as he's making money and nobody grasses him up"

Anyway, Shane walked in the shop with a motorbike helmet and spurted out a list of what he was wanting. The drink was behind the counter, and the shop looked more like a fish tank, where there was plastic windows all around so ye couldn't touch any of the drink" Baba knew he was probably underage, but he never cared eh. Shane probably never had a pube to his name eh, pubeless cunt.

Shane tried to memorise what he needed. 2 blue bags later Shane walked out the shop looking like the man, the hero. Fuckin everyone knows, Shane was the boy. He carried the bottles of drink down the street, clink, clink, and clink. Then all of a sudden, saw a riot van at the top of the street going past. Dale was like, "Aww, the fuckin bizzies"

The riot van stopped, reversed back and started heading down the street. They took off, for Shane; all he could hear was clink, clink, clink, and he was hoping 'dinnae let the bags burst, dinnae let the bags burst'. The van was getting closer where they ran over to the wasteland, to the hill. He ran up to the top of the hill where he jumped in the hole and ducked down. The riot van stopped at the wasteland. The bizzies got out and with a torch and started scanning over. All they could see was the hole; they couldn't see them inside the hill. Ryan had a good plan. After a couple minutes they could hear the walkie talkies making the noise going 'chgrrrgh, and thought we were gonna get caught'.

Their eyes were peering out the hole, the police never seen them. They left and the boys waited a couple more minutes. Then they finally arrived at the park, looking like the heroes they are eh.

Chelsea went, "why did it take you so long?"

"Aw we just got chased by the bizzies" said Dale.

Anyway, the party in the park began, doing dizzy lizzies with a bottle of bucky and playing pitchy and flirting with the lassies. Ryan's best chat up line to the lassies was,

"ye want to see ma hole?" They never knew what he was on about, just thought he was a dirty bastard eh. Just smoking dope and just wanting a grope, they tried to get a game of dares on the go. Dave dared Shantelle to bag off with Dale, Shantelle turned around and said,

"Naw, he's a smelly bastard." Everyone laughed eh, but it was a shame on Dale. Shane thought *'shit this is gonna be my turn'*. Dale thought to dare Shane to go home, who told him to fuck off eh,

"I still got half a bottle to go, and I'm no going hame yet". He was red faced but it was a laugh.

Tam was out his shell, started flashing everybody, showing how big his balls were. People were screaming and laughing, fuckin Tam. Quietest one there eh but he's swinging his banger, knowing he probably had the biggest banger there. That was his party trick, trying to do a weapons catch by flicking it in the air and grabbing it between his legs, and then showing everybody a fruit bowl where his arse is oot, his balls are hanging oot the back and his toot it in the middle. I know; weird fuckin night.

Dale and Ryan thought it would be a good idea to walk along the street kicking car wing mirrors off and jumping on the roofs. Ryan slipped and cracked the window of a car. They legged it, and the drinks were gone; nobody got anything that night. Was all mouth and nobody got their hole like they said eh.

Like I say, nobody got smelly fingers that night. It's just hope n dreams, nights they were gonna mind for years to come. When yer sitting in a park freezing cold where yer fuckin willy is probably all shrivelled up an it would be embarrassing if ye even let her put her hand doon yer pants. That was the type of nights it was, but definitely the nights you were gonna remember.

Chapter 4: Still in school

They were in art. Arts a good laugh. Art ye can fuck about. Shane was quite good wi art, that's where he was creative. It was him and Chris Clarkling that was sitting, chilling in the back of class. Chris brought out a lump of hash, honestly was nearly the size of his palm. Johns like

"Is that hash?"

"Aye" said Chris.

goes "fuck that's looks like boot polish mate, honestly look at the size of it, it's probably got
thing in it, probably all boot polish and plastic"

nyway, Chris started burning it in class, the smoke was rising up. The teacher; Mr Gardener opens
e door where he got a big old whiff of "wacky baccy" what Mr Gardener would say. Chris quickly
it it in his pocket before Mr Gardener seen it. Shane could see the smoke still rising up, but Mr
rdener's eyes couldn't see it.

nyway the bell rang and they went to a different class. John was in most of Shanes classes, he sat
xt to John and he was with the lassies. He was quite a popular man, lassies liked his chat. You
ow, he was a bit of a mouth piece; he knew had the gift of the gab sort of thing, he knew he had
big himself up. Whereas Shane never. Shane was kind of more honest that way, he never felt as
od saying it. He couldn't big himself up, just kind of more honest that way. Anyway they were
ting next to the lassies, this is where Shane seen a different side of John. John started taking Shane
wn to boost himself up in front of the lassies.

mind when ye used to be a wee sweaty, an a little Goth with yer slipknot t-shirt on" said John.
is is a change of scene with John, before this he was sound as. He seemed not so interested in
ane. Well, we already know he's fuckin with a couple lassies in the class that were popular at the
ne.

hn pointed at Shanes trackies, "What's that? Fuckin 4 stripes? Never heard of 4 stripes. A heard a
stripe before eh, but 4 stripes?" and the lassies laughed

e goes, "What type of trainers are they?" and pointed at the make.

that Lonsdale trainers?" said John, "no Adidas naw?" The lassies laughed.

Honestly how poor are ye by the way?" Shane said nothing he was building up anger, they were
ughing, making a fool, made him look like he was poor.

hn was with the lassies,

ve got a joint" they said,

When did ye get that?"

w just in art, rolled it in there. Fancy coming round the back of the bike sheds and we smoke it
ter the class?"

e bell went and that's what happened, everyone had a smoke. Shane never, Shane just stood
ere like a fly on the wall.

ey all ended up going to English. They're sitting in class; again Shane was in one next to John. The
ssie were sitting behind us, as one of them got a fit of giggles. Dunno how as it was hash at the end
the day and wasny like grass. But she kept on giggling and giggling and making it fuckin obvious
hat she was smoking. John was like, "Pipe doon eh, yer gonna get us caught"

nyway the teacher was coming up. They all used to call her Lizzie tin tits, cause she had massive
ngers. Ye could see her nipples that were like hard as fuckin bullets. Anyway that was Shane

describing Lizzie tin tits. She was handing us all a piece of paper and she went up to the lassie that couldn't not stop laughing, and they were getting paranoid thinking they were gonna get caught. This lassies name was Beejee, some of the guys used to call her gobbles. Anyway, that was the end eh fuckin English that day. Shane was walking along for his next class.

Chapter 5: Couple months has went past

A couple of months had gone past. Even Shane thought John was cool, and kept him on benefit of the doubt. There were bits of him where he just realised he's a user in his own way. Not all the time Shane used to shrug it off and think about the other decent bits aboot him. Thing is, this is the day where it started to change.

Shane and John were in woodwork, with Mr Gallagher. Mr Gallagher never used to take any pish o the boys in woodwork and so Chrissy finished off his project. His project, he made a baseball bat. M Gallagher went, "where is it you live Christopher?"

He said, "Hillhouse"

"Well, yer no gettin that" and then he disposed of his baseball bat, which he was making for 2 wee solid.

"Shane can you pass me that Stanley knife" said Mr Gallagher.

Shane took the Stanley knife and chucked it on the table, not aggressively, but just put it on the table.

Mr Gallagher went and said, "you tryna hit me with that knife?"

Shanes like, "naw, you were wanting the knife. I passed it to ye"

"Get out ma class!"

Shane sat in the class by himself for the rest of the day, just because of Mr Gallagher. The teacher took a disliking to Shane, for some reason. Maybe he thought Shane was the ring leader cause he was bigger before realising it was John the mouthpiece who was ring leader. Anyway Shane, a couple weeks later, was allowed back into Mr Gallaghers class again as Shane and John was tasked with painting a chair. Missing the chair completely, John painted "YND", right on the middle of the classroom wall. Anyway it was gonna be one out of the two of them that was caught for this.

John said "Honestly can you take the rap for me, cause I'm already on a yellow card"

"Well why did ye do it?" said Shane

"Aw just take it, you dinnae have a yellow card." Anyway Shane being daft ended up doing it. That was it. Mr Gallagher went mental at Shane, lost the fuckin head. Shane took it the ballicking and it went right through one ear and out the other, he wasny caring. He wasn't allowed back in for that whole year; that was him needing to spend the time out of that class. John never even said thanks for it.

the weekend, Shane thought he'd go to Johns bit, because he asked him.

John says, "After school, ye can just come and stay over at mines" so Shane did. They started speaking about what they'd get up to on the weekend.

Chapter 6: Baby faced and Under Aged

John asked Shane, "Come to ma bit this weekend, ye can stay over and my brother can get us in the club. Bring least aboot 20 quid". When you're that age ye think 20 quid is a lot of money then ye realise you are gonna get laughed at as you go for a round and realise ye don't have enough money. Anyway they never knew that at the time.

After school on a Friday they ended up going to Johns house. John's was on the borderline. There was a rough area across the road from him, but his house was actually alright. It was quite a nice looking hoose, was still in a dodgy area. You know the shops is a no man's land sort of thing.

Shane by this point was a bit wary of John eh, you know, thinking about Mr Gallagher and he never passed John up for it. He was just in a class by himself for the next wee while, and got shifted to the blue huts with all the rest of the happy bunnies. That's not where Shane was wanting to be and Shane used to sit on top of the roof at Asda and skive that class. Anyway it was in the back of his mind, but he went along to John's hoose anyway.

He arrived at John's door and Shane seen John's dad. John used to tell Shane stories his dad was a face of the city, where he was a well-known guy. He looked like he never left the 80s, still a skinhead, you know he just looked like he had a boxers face. I don't know how much of the stories aboot what John told Shane was true about his dad, but aye he looked like a bulldog, and that's probably why John was trying to act up in his dad's shoes sort of thing. Anyway, his dad was happy to sit around and spraff away his stories to Shane, telling him about the good old days of football.

"Aye a used to go about with an umbrella, used to sharpen the end of ma umbrella" said John's dad.

"that'd be ma fuckin weapon. Best days when we ran on the pitch and battered fuck oot the Aberdeen casuals but that was a good 20 odd year ago by this point. Ye listen to it when it's an older man telling ye this, an John looking proud because his dad was a so called hard man. John's dad looked like Vinny Jones a wee bit.

Johns like, "go show us the scar dad, the one when you were fighting with those 2 guys"

"Aw with a machete?" you know, with a smug look on his face. Anyway he showed them it. *Yeah it was a battle scar* is what Shane thought. It was more just to boost up the stories of what Johns been telling all the school, a how mental and hard his dad is eh.

"Anyway boys you going out drinking tonight?"

"Aye"

"Aye, your brothers taking you down to the fuckin gunner?"

"Aye" said John. They got dressed, put on shirts and tried to look older than what they are. 8 o'cloc came, and they used fake ID that John's got. It wasny gonna work, looked like he sellotaped a pictu over card, but they were gonna take it anyway.

John's brother arrived "right boys, you coming out for a drink then?"

They were walking down the street, and there was a pub with a flat roof, and it had very little windows; just wee windows at the top. That should have been alarm bells straight away, not to dri in the gunner. Just got outside and the door got swung open, a guy went stumbling out it and another guy, think it was the barman, was waving a baseball bat, "yer not coming fuckin back in he again eh!" Just when he said it they thought fuck this and went to another pub. There was no way they were getting in there. They went to the Gilly on the corner. The 'Gilly' was an old man's pub, there was no banter, and no craic and nothing happening. Shane started drinking and downing the pints thinking *"ah this is quite cool were sitting in a pub just wait till the boys hear about this and what a was up to on the weekend"*.

Now Dave, Ryan, Dale and Tam were drinking in the park over the other side of the city. Dave's in the park chancing Shantelle. She already heard from Chelsea about his fuckin small willy and he couldn't get it up, that was him fucked. But he was trying like a trooper any, God loves a trier devil likes a chancer.

Anyway they were over the other side of the city, in John's area, on Friday night. Where they heard shouting and roaring coming. They thought well this is excitement, what's happening here. It was o firm day and they were in an area next to the football stadium. There was a big fight happening outside the pub where people were rolling around the ground fuckin looking like something out of fuckin UFC, people were getting jumped about. There was a group of guys just at the pub door where one man coming flying over with a karate kick straight oot of Bruce Lees fuckin soul. The res of the boys, they seen this, and these were grown men rolling aboot fuckin fighting about football eh. Tam, the quiet guy you always gotta watch out for, took off his belt and thought he could get in bit of this and show how hard he is eh. Swinging his belt about and dancing on the street no really doing much, just roaring and shouting cause this is the young team isn't it. Not a moment too soon they see a guy getting bottled where he was gushing blood. Shane's mates did nothing, just stood and watched after Tam sort of piped doon and realised he's no running into that. They watched till the riot van pulled up, police were in riot gear and started huddling everybody, they thought they would give a quick exit and fuck off.

Shane on the other side of the city, was sitting there staring at a packet of peanuts fuckin daydreaming because there was fuck all happening in this pub. A don't think even a women's ever been in this pub. Shane watched a guy pished, and started trying to dance before walking over to another guy and dry humping him. That was Shane's excitement of the night.

Chapter 7: Spraffin Shite

Shane and Dave went round to Dave's brothers flat, Coco.

They started speaking about the weekend, "Ah was hearing yer fighting in the weekend with the big guys over the football."

Dave was like, "Aye, you know ye should a seen it" He started telling all the stories, honestly sounded like suttin out a movie the way Dave was going on about it.

Coco was here, "A was hearing about big Tam, big raj Tam fuckin takin off his belt an jumping about"

Shane heard the truth later on; Tam did take off his belt and was jumping about hoping it would impress the lassies. You know actin like a peacock, just being loud and dancing on the curb, a curb dancer really.

Anyway, Dave was telling them all the stories and then Shane started talking about his weekend going on,

"Aw I was out at the pub" you know trying to look cool,

"I was down at the gunner, seen a guy get chased oot with a baseball bat" fuckin exaggerating saying he was covered in blood when he wasny really eh just got fuckin huddled out the door,

"Then a met with Johns dad, aye he's a gangster"

Coco goes "what he thinks he a gangster, that guy naw, he thinks he's a gangster"

Then Shane tried to boost up his story by saying "naw he showed me a slash mark that he got with a machete"

Coco started laughing' he goes,

"You think that's a slash mark, I'll show ye what a fuckin slash mark looks like" and pointed at his face. Yeh okay his face did look a bit like chucky, with all these battle scars.

"That's a fuckin slash mark. John's dad so called gangster aye okay. You know, probably got it in jail when he was gonna get raped" that's what Coco said.

Anyway Shane started to think. He's started to be more like his mates; starting to talk shite, you know, making out like he's a so called hard man himself. The stories he's telling, he's not even been involved in them, he's just seen more people pull doon their fuckin trousers and show him fuckin slash marks and stab marks. Yeah it wasny lies but he was painting himself out to be a fuckin hard man eh.

They rolled up a joint and this time even Shane took a puff. Coco took out a video box which was full of weed and skins. They rolled it up and puffed it and passed it along. Coco seemed alright, he seemed a bit edgy you know, that's probably where Dave gets it from. Coco kept on calling Dave 'Disco'.

Shane went, "Why ye get called disco?"

and he went "Disco Dave"

"Aw that makes sense, fair enough" means Dave was now Disco Dave.

They were walking down the street at night, just Shane and Dave. Or now Disco Dave as we found out. They see Shantelle and Chelsea.
"Alright?"

They were looking over at a block of flats on fire, they see the fire engine go past. Was probably little bams what lit it on fire. These are abandoned flats, council kind of take a blind eye to it, they want it to go on fire, means it's easier to knock it down. They dinnae condone it but do take a blind eye to it Bonfire night, why build a bonfire when there's old derelict flats there to burn down. Anyway they watched that for a wee while and then headed home.

Chapter 8: Driving

Before the internet to buy anything used you go to Scotmid and you look on the noticeboard and there'd be yellow bits of paper written "stuff for sale, second hand". Well, they were looking through it one day and it would be scrapheap cars. Shane phoned them up and then Dave went roond and picked the car up. Shane one night, was waiting outside the park where Dave pulled over in the car. Honestly it had kangaroo petrol, fuckin Dave couldn't drive to save himself. Anyway, Shane, Dave, Ryan, Tam and smelly Dale were all crammed in this car. Now that was too many in the car already. Cruising down the road thinking they're cool as fuck. Honestly this car was jailbait, they were gonna get pulled over at any minute as the axel was gonna drop out it, this thing wasny gonna last long eh.

Here was Shantelle, Chelsea and Sarah-Jane. They pulled up thinking *we're the boys*.

"Where did you get the fuckin shite heap?" said Chelsea.

"We bought it. What ye want to come for a cruise?" Now; far too many people in the car by this point. Fuckin looking more like a clown car, the windows were steaming up. Shantelle sat on Shane's knee, he wasny complaining eh.

"That better not be a stiffy I'm feeling" said Shantelle to Shane.

"Naw" but it was.

Anyway, Smelly Dale took over driving cause Dave couldn't drive to save himself, like I said. They bombed down the road going fuckin 25 miles an hour. They went doon the street, roond the corner, and roond the car park twice, then black smoke started pouring out it. That was it; it was over. The car was done. Smelly Dale opened up the bonnet and says;

"Aye it's fucked"

I dinny know if Dale knew what he was doing eh but he was looking like the man. They took the number plates off and fuckin tanned the windows and left it lying there. Then next week they got the yellow papers and they done it all over again.

ey got this car what looked better than the last one, I mean just better than the last one. They
ed in and again got the lassies, but it was only Shantelle and Chelsea this time. Dale, he was trying
do a handbrake turn when Chelsea started crying and screaming.

top it you're gonna end up crashing" they just laughed; they thought they knew what they were
ing. Then the police went past. Now their hearts all fuckin sank at this moment, hadn't been in the
r 10 minutes till this happened. The police went past they never stopped, it seemed all good. They
re going round the streets fuckin listening to gangster rap thinking they're cool.

here's my ma" said Ryan. Dale thought it would be smart and beeped the horn then they all
cked. The car must have gone past looking like nobody was driving it. At this point it was getting a
risky, going round and round the streets, they never went out the area like. They ditched the car
the wasteland. They got a cloth, stuck it in the petrol tank and then lit it. Anyway that was their
y over.

apter 9: Summer Holidays

yway summer holidays arrived, as did gang fighting. That's what happened. Don't know if it's the
t weather or basic boredom or if it was Ryan shagging another person's Mrs and they were after
m. Or was it smelly Dale spray painting' on the walls of the shops saying "Sanders likes the boaby".
ey would have loved to seen his face, when he seen it, if that were true. Anyway it was happening.

ane and Dave were in Dave's room, showing him his makeshift nun chucks. Basically a mop
apped in two with a chain nailed to it. They were all meeting up at the back of the shops, other
ys from other areas came to join up with them to fight the YMB. Stashing golf clubs in bushes and
eryone was tooled up. Was like a normal night; lassies were there, everyone was drinking to the
int they forgot what they're there for. Everyone actin like the tinman, and fuckin thinking they're
e hardest thing about. You know, shouting and roaring, and speaking about stories about fighting.
m comes along walking like he's got a limp, pulls out a fuckin samurai.

What the fuck ye gonna do with that Tam? Looking like you just bought it from Baba's cave" He
oked the part, you wouldn't go anywhere near him like.

uckin hell Tam, what ye doing with this, fuckin wee grinder thing"

ey started telling stories about the last time wi Tam, when he went and bought a crossbow an
ot it at the YMB. Missed em like, but tell you what I guarantee they fuckin went and touched cloth
hen that went spinning past there heed.

hen everyone was showing what tools they got, Dale pulled out a football sock. Dave was like
vhit ye gonna do with that?"

w am gonna put two snooker balls in it" said Dale, "am no gonna run up an go aw smell ma socks"

ye ye definitely knock em out wi that, wouldn't ye Dale?"

w shut it!"

Anyway they're all drinking and walking down to the park, down to the river where there was a bridge. They were still drinking, carrying on, and after a while end up forgetting what was about to happen. You know, they were having a good time. Thing is: it's nothing like the movies. It's no organised enough like when groups meet at a specific time then ye fight in a tunnel.

Davy was chancing the lassies, making em oot like he was the fuckin big man. Later on, everyone h a bevvie, everyone was drunk, they were saying the YMB was just a bunch of fucking paps. A no show. There no coming eh.

A group of boys came along and they mingled in with us although Shanes thinking *these are faces I haven't seen*.

One guy came up, he goes, "where ye fae?" to Shane.

Shane said, "Hillburn"

"Aye well fuckin ma cousin stays in Hillburn an you should come along with us like" Seemed friendl enough.

An the boy standing next to the back of Shane says "am from Hillburn as well"

"Are ye, aye?" Shane replies sarcastically.

Out of nowhere the boy behind Shane got sucker punch to the point that one punch cleared 2 people oot, as he fell on top of another. He was put on his arse. Shane froze *what the fuck*. In that split moment the YMB was in amongst us. Everything was kicking off by that point people were launching bottles and bricks. People started to scatter. The group started to disperse due curb dancing and bouncing aboot.

Anyway, Davy was lying on a grass verge next to the river. Felt like it was only a split second that th all kicked off. One minute speaking to the lassies the next minute he's got sparkled in the moof anc pushed right in the river. Shane ran along and tried to pull him up. People are getting stomped on and just swinging windmill punches more in hope than anything else, the adrenaline kicking in.

The team that came with them, they started fleeing. They're all talk; all fart and no shit. They didn' even stand their ground. Shane didn't know what to do, but fished Davy oot and started running along the river with the rest of them.

 Shane shouts, "Where's Tam?"

Davy handed him his knuckle dusters and says, "I'm no going back, fuck that"

Shane grabbed Davys knuckle dusters and ran back doon the canal to see Tam chasing two boys wi that fucking samurai. Like a big game of chase me chase me. Neighbours on their balcony, egging e on shouting; "No cunts stabbing any cunt! Am gonna kick yer cunt in when I get doon there! Why watch Eastenders or soaps when this is happening outside yer window on a Saturday night."

ane started chasing Tam; trying to catch up to him but at that moment, Tam gets smacked on the ck of the heid with a stick by one of the other boys, and they all surround him. Tam's waving this ckin samurai, nobody was going anywhere near him but it did create an opening to leg it, meeting ane as they both took toes. Tam couldn't resist in shouting abuse as they both made their escape.

e other boys were shouting "Yer getting stabbed!" to Tam, while Tam was the one holding the murai. Tam and Shane started to flee back from it. It was all shouting and fuckin throwing punches the wind. It was a mess, a quiet riot. At that moment the riot van pulled up. It was getting broken ▪, everyone was running in different directions, it never lasted long. But yeah, that was the turday night.

vy said "least a got a sore face instead of a red face an never ran away"

ane was just thinking *well I was the one who ran back for Tam*, but he never said anything about at.

le and Ryan were alright, just full of adrenaline, and thought this was brilliant fun. The rest of the ys from school, they were all jus mouthpieces. Done fuck all eh, instead of getting slapped about, ey all fuckin left when it got too heavy.

apter 10: Round the back of the bike sheds

le, John and Chrissy just finished art class; they went roond the back of the bike sheds, the usual. e of Shanes old mates, you know, skater type and the hardest boy in school, was starting on him. w you dinny want to be starting on this guy man, Aaron Thomson. This guy looks like a eanderthal; he's got a mono-brow and the most evil eyes on him.

yway, he was starting on Shane's old mate. Shane walked over with John and Chrissy, dunno what was all aboot, but Shane didny notice that Aaron was carrying a knife in his hand, threatening the her boy. He wasn't going to do anything, just threatening him, making his presence known. Even if ▪ wasn't going to do fuck all, he was still shitting it.

ane said to Aaron "just leave it man" before pulling him away. Aaron's ego seemed a bit bounced om this, "who do the fuck do you hink you are?"

aron soon walked away and John said,

"ou shouldn't have stepped in there"

thought he'd just walk away, even if he had a reputation for being the hardest boy in school"

ane didn't think much about it after. After their fag, they walked into the shops to get a mars bar d a roll. This was to be their lunch, along with a can of 'Shandy' or a glass bottle of 'Irn Bru'. rissy was walking past a car, when he noticed the window slightly open, he thought he could try shing it further down. He put his sleeves over his hands and used his body weight to push it down ore. "Bingo" he says as it went down enough to crawl in and then out, returning with a pair of sunglasses and a Steps CD, face beaming like he's just scored a jackpot. The others weren't much impressed. *What the fuck was the point in that?* But that was Chrissy, if it's not nailed down, it's getting taken. Type of guy that would steal the sugar out your tea.

Anyway, the bell rang and we headed back to class. Shane was walking in the corridor and he seen Aaron. Aaron came up to him,

"Do you hink you're hard aye?"

"What you on about" asks Shane

"Do you hink you're fucking hard" Aaron asks again. Shane didn't know how to answer that but replied "naw".

John and Chrissy were behind him but said nothing.

"Aw so do you think you're a fucking pap then aye, you're no hard naw?" said Aaron, trying to start him up.

Shanes thought was if he had to fight, may as well be in school where there's teachers to break it up. Shane didn't fancy his chances with him. If it kicks off, teachers will stop it. So Shane started to get bit wide. Not to look cool just to get it over with. In Shanes head this will be done and dusted within seconds.

"I'm harder than the guy looking at me anyways" said Shane. "Fuck it, we're fighting after school" said Aaron, by this point the teacher had already shouted at us to get into class. John was sitting next to Shane

"You gonna be easy about him?"

"What do you mean?" asked Shane,

"You're fighting him after school so you easy about him?" asks John.

"I've nout against the guy "said Shane,

"Aye but you've got to stand up for yourself" said John.

Shane now was thinking this is the last subject in the school day. Maybe if he gets out quick, back home and by tomorrow it'll all be forgotten about? The bell rang and John wasn't having it – Shane leaving early. After class John went up to Aaron and started saying

"Shane thinks you're soft and he's gonna take you"

"Is that right aye?" says Aaron,

"Aye he says he's fucking easy about fighting you, Shanes wondering if it's going to be at the park after".

Shane is soon on his on his way home when John runs up next to him "what you doing, you're going the wrong way, you're meant to be going to the park"

Now by this point John, Shane and Chrissy were all walking to the park; Shane didn't know what to think. The whole school came along; we could have honestly sold tickets. Even the teachers were in the background looking on, making sure the fight was away from school premises and after you walk over the road from the school, they soon left. This was box office, a massive group of laddies and lassies came to see this fight. Aaron went in first through the gates, as everyone is standing by the side, whole group chanting.

People were coming up to Shane passing on fighting advice "just do this big man, 1 2 1 2"

Shane had change in his pocket which was crunched in his fist to help reinforce it. Then Shane thought, he doesn't want to fight dirty in a square go, if he's gonna fight it should be a clean square go.

The chants started by everyone "fight, fight, fight"

Shane had no anger towards this guy and couldn't just snap into it. Aaron threw a left hook, which was like being hit by a sledgehammer. One minute Shane was staring straight on, the next – staring to the right. Then he got hit with a left before Shane sussed he needs to hit this guy. Shane put him in a headlock, wrestled for a second but got out it. Shane still didn't have the aggression or anger to hit this guy and his bottle was going. The whole school was watching on, shouting,

"Fucking hit him!"

Aaron was running around looking like a boxer and clocked Shane right in the mouth, with his lip turning up like Elvis. It wasn't much a fight. Ye, Shane never went down, but he didn't really hit back either. He bottled it, pride gone, in front of the entire school; Shane was a joke, a loser. When he was leaving the park, Shane didn't want to face school again tomorrow. He felt nobody would have any respect for him anymore, possibly they never did anyway. Aaron walked away with a group of guys thinking he was the coolest thing, whilst Shane walked the other way.

Shane went back to school the next day; he was filled with anger at this point. He felt embarrassed, like his pride has been taken away from him. One boy came up to him,

"Where's the black eye?" Shane didn't have any black eyes. John was acting smart in front of the older lads,

"Oh please don't hurt my face" letting people know how the fight went down.

Shane said "I never said that" as John laughed.

"You win some, you lose some" said John.

"You know Aaron feels bad about yesterday, he wants to make it up to you" as John and Shane walked.

"Fuck that, I'm no making up with him" says Shane.

It's not like Shane wanted people to think he was hard or scared of him but everything changed after that. Things like walking into the shop. They used to just walk in, skip the queue, but Shane didn't. He'd queue politely; even the goths and skaters weren't intimated by him. Shane had no respect, but Shane wasn't seeking that anyway.

Chapter 12 – Partying

Ryan had a free house this weekend which they all planned. They needed drink, Dave wanted the lassies up, it's gonna be mental. Dave organised how to get lassies, the others organised how to get the drink for the house. They all headed down to the Somerfield, although none of us really had much money. Shane went in first, he wasn't a tea leaf, and he was going to go in for a lookout. Dale went in second, with the security guard following because he looks dodgy as fuck. Ryan, Tam and Dave went in after. Shane stayed at the top of aisle, keeping a lookout whilst they went to the alcohol aisle and slyly put bottles of vodka up their sleeve. They walked out and Shane was sweating, like a peado in a park, worried in case they get caught. They went out, stashed the vodka and went back in. If it worked the first time, it'll work again. They done this twice then swiftly left with around £40 of drink. Party is on.

They pull up to the house, with vodka in hand, but no fanny inside. Well, plenty of fannies but nae lassies, just a sausage fest. They all chipped in to rolling a joint. Dale had soapy, Dave had grass and Tam had some soft black. They crumbled it in, mixed it and had a hybrid Bob Marley joint, using a bucket as an ashtray, burning away for hours. Dave's brother, Coco, turned up and then eventually some lassies turned up after.

The party is underway, music is banging, some DJ Rankin and DJ Cammie, the happy hard core you used to listen to. Sideshow music was blasting. Coco was alrite, he was a bit older than us, bit more edgy, and he was in the corner chatting up the lassies. Ryan was fucking steaming; he bounced off every wall just to make it to the toilet. Nobody saw him for hours. Shane by this point was getting pretty boozy, bit drunk and seen Ryan lying on the floor hugging the toilet.

"Come on now Ryan eh, fucking move" whilst trying to take a pish.

Ryan wasn't for budging, whilst Shane was focussing on aiming straight into the toilet it's harder than it looks when drunk. Stumbling and aiming up but the pish was going everywhere and hit Ryan, although Ryan barely moved. He never meant to pish on Ryan but when trying to aim straight again, he fell into the bath, like a fountain, pish spraying up everywhere. He got up and stumbled out, covered in piss but Shane wasn't caring. Ryan was still hugging the pan at this point. He got in the hallway, one minute standing up; the next lying down having face planted the ground. This wisnae too bad cause the lassies were going to the toilet and Shane had a good view when they walked over him.

Shane got up and crashed on the couch, maybe he's whitied, maybe it's the drink. Two things that never mix well; weed and drink.

Ryan floated in, "wheey, party's still on!" not realising he was still covered in pish.

ere was a bowl of crisps on the table, "aww, I'm gonnae be sick" muttered Ryan before spewing in
e crisp bowl.

eryone shouted "Ewww, you manky bastard!"

an apologised "I'm sorry, I never meant it. At least it's not on the carpet"

eryone forgot about what Ryan had done to the crisps until the next day when the munchies hit
d they started snacking on them. Everyone was boaking.

/hat's wrong?"

ucking Ryan spewed in the crisps"

an piped up "it's no my sick, what you on about? I never spewed in the crisp, that's dip". It was
o late, everyone by that point was being sick.

ey're outside the house, having heart-to-hearts and chatting shite when a boy approached the
ont of the house. He was shouting "YMD!" and holding a meat cleaver.

/hat the fuck! Who's this guy?"

ople are looking out the window. It was just this one boy, steaming and shouting "YMD".

e headed back in to the house, "there's a boy out there, fucking off his nut screaming YMD".

of a sudden, you could hear the chant "who are we, we're the mental YMD. With a baseball bat
d a snooker cue, we're gonna fucking leather you"

ere was a whole team of them, he must have got note that there was a party here. They quickly
ed to close the door as they were trying to boot the door open. The fear was getting to them now,
ey were really fucking stoned. Chantel was absolutely shitting it. They started putting blades
rough the letterbox, swinging it back and forth while continuing to bang and kick the door.

/hat the fuck are we going to do?"

e only time Shane has enjoyed seeing the Police was when they pulled up and the YMD boys
attered. That was the end of that party, a lot of mess and a lot of hangovers.

IAPTER 13: Bored through the week

ane went up to Dale's flat, no slagging here but you could smell the poverty in the flat. The basic
sentials were missing, like no carpet on the floor and no washing machine. He did have a
ayStation and a TV and running council juice from the taps, so we were sorted for water and
ming. No complaints, that's just how it was. They got bored playing the PlayStation so Shane
oned Dave to see where he was. They were all hanging out by the shops.

ancy going out?" said Shane to Dale.

ye, fuck it. Let's just go" was Dale's response.

They left and headed to the shops. Whilst sitting there and hanging about, Coco and his friend turned up.

"What happened at the weekend when I left? I heard the YMD came along"

Shane told them the story of the evening, what had happened. Coco responded

"That was all my doing boys, eh. They're fucking after me after a couple weeks ago. Anyway, we're going up there in a couple of weeks to kick one of their cunts in for thinking they can come down and start a fight"

That was Coco, he wasnae letting it go. Coco and his mate headed off. I think he is going to batter one of the boys.

The dark nights were setting upon them; the winter was just around the corner. They were walking the street where they knew a paedophile lived. It was like a modern day witch hunt. You can do anything and justify it because he is a peado. They were taunting him as he came to the window and Dale was messing about "You want this" and showing him his hairy arse.

Dave was like "Fucking put that away man. He's going to end up bumming you".

The guy came out; it was just for a chase. He started chasing us while Dale was trying to pull up his trousers but all Shane could see was his bare arse in the night while he was running away. They thought it was a great laugh and kept on going back there. They done it the next night and started chucking staines at his window, booted his door and left a bin against it so when he his door the bin falls in and his rubbish and shit going everywhere.

They got bored of that quickly. A few days later Tam took some fireworks. These weren't fireworks, they were bombs; they were fucking bam fireworks. They got creative with what to do with them. Let one off and it was a banger, chucked it at a window where a so called prostitute lived. It made huge bang and then they chucked another one and hid behind a bush.

She opened the window "What the fuck was that?!"

"That must be one of your clients, hen" they responded before running away laughing.

They stuck one on an electric box and lit it and ran down a close, the explosion sounded like a bomb went off. It never did much to the metal electric box but the bang was loud enough. Stuck one on a parked car, on the exhaust but it never went off. Stupidly Dave went back and stuck another banger on the windshield, it went off and it shattered the window. They still had rockets.

There was a shite bin where people but their dogs waste in, they stuck one in and were waiting but never went off. As a man and his dog walked passed, it exploded and went fucking everywhere. The bin was in bits, shite was up the trees and the guy probably shat himself as well because we definitely did. They ran away laughing like wee fucking school girls when Dave thought it would be funny to lay a rocket on the ground and then shoot it going straight towards us. We're running, screaming but thinking this was a good carry on and all of a sudden you hear the whizzing of it as the rocket took off. It missed us as we were running down the street. Even after the flash and bang I could still hear Tam's heavy footstep with his 'Rockport's' still running away.

ey end back at Shane's flat thinking of ways to get more money to get more fireworks as it was a od carry on. They upped the stakes and thought of more ideas, it's just boredom in the winter. m started telling the story of last year of how he went on top of the shops roof and lit a wheelie n on fire, someone phoned the fire brigade. They were all there waiting as Tam lit a petrol bomb, ened to a Molotov, before throwing it in front of the fire engine as it was approaching.

ucking mental" said Shane,

ye but it was a good chase though eh". So they started speaking about stories like these, pish chat.

apter 14: It got serious.

co was walking home one night through the old railway when he got jumped by a group of boys m the YMD. He got stomped on, there was a load of them, and they just left him there. Shane and le were walking home that night when they see an ambulance going past, they thought nothing of It wasn't until the day after that they found out; it was Coco who got stabbed. It never took them ng to figure out what boys did it and that was them, in jail and for what? All over our area they ere mouthing off, looking hard for being a tool merchant.

ane was back at school, it was registration. John was noising him up which got to the point that ane was fucked off with him now, he had seen who John was now and he wasn't a mate. John was owing off in front of the lassies.

Vhat kinda team does Hillburn have" said John,

lobody knows who Hillburn are eh"

was the YMD who were top boys around there. It wasn't that Shane was too bothered about what hn was saying, he was just trying to put him down in front of the lassies and they were hoovering it , all laughing with John.

ucking look at you eh, can you even fight?" asked John. Shane didn't even have a thought process, just took over. He jumped out his seat, rugby tackled him and started punching him and stomping d kicking his face before walking out of registration. The teacher never knew what to do. The ssies were all looking at John, just been kicked in.

ane left school and skived that day, thinking he's bound to have been thrown out. Next day he ent back, John seemed sheepish before apologising to Shane,

was only having a laugh"

he whole time aye?" said Shane.

hn suddenly wanted to be Shane's mate; Shane brushed it off and dropped it. It wasn't Shane who ded up on the ground covered in blood.

Chapter 15: Devilment.

They all went out that night. It was winter, everyone had their beanies on and scarves wrapped around their face. They all went round to local peado to throw stones at his window, to get a chase. He came out, started chasing them. Dale, Dave and Shane got round the corner first, like a whippet on speed but Ryan got caught. Ryan threw a punch and just clipped him, tried to do it again but the guy caught his arm. Tam went up behind the guy and pulled out a blunt axe, hitting him to the side of the face, liberties taking it too far. They ran away and ended up back in Shane's house.

Shane was sweating, not believing what they did. Dave seemed not too bothered about it. It was taken way too far. It was only meant to be a laugh, now he's got a mars bar (scar) down his face. For days, Shane was shitting his self, *what happens if the police come to the door? What do I say?* The guy was alrite though and nobody got in trouble for it. The peado eventually moved house after the attack.

Shane started to break away from the group, started seeing sense, realising none of this was fun anymore, and it was more about fitting in, finding his place. He'd see his friends sitting in the stairs at night and he'd rather sit in at home and do his own thing. Drinking in the park because it was a Friday became shite, the girls would hang with guys in their cars, usual sausage fest. Shane sat in his house and broke away from it all. It was the last few weeks of school; he'll get to drop this shithole soon too.

After a year or so had passed, Tam found he never grew up, he was in and out of prison, like his own bed and breakfast cause deep down he was violent. Last I heard about Ryan was he tried to rob a bakers with his ma's tights on his face, running out with money in the till and tripped. He got caught and was in and out of there. Dale grew up and away, starting as a labourer and then working in a trade, a brickie. He had himself a bird and even a wee car, he was doing well. Dave, disco Dave, well he enjoyed the marching powder too much, it had changed him, and people couldn't be fucked with him anymore now, so I got told. He was that para when going down to McDonalds, he'd get his mates carrying golf clubs as security just to get a burger. What did Shane do? Well, Shane wrote a book about it all.

Ghost writers: Emma, Imogen & Jamie

this is how I wrote my story in high

school looking like a comic book

that morning eating my
coco pops. There was
a knock on the door.

Davie was at
the door

are you comming Skate
Ja Ja

Pull your trousers up
you scatty basterds

your ma

Do your fucking
getting it. Come
doun mking you
know cto his brolur is

1411 right Davi
sound.

thats whats good
about being with
Dav everyone know
his brother so
no body will start.

Dave was
speaking about
his brother having
tt police arested
him got him in th
back off riel van

and beters
fuck out of
him

O Shit

Dave was asking what we were going to do in the summer holidays

I said I would be going back North to visit my family

I don't think Dav was happy but said nothing

2 months later after summer holidays

haven't seen Dav since I was back.

there was a boy in the stair well dressing with a burbery cap

All right pal when did you get back said Dav. Summer time I was hanging around with my brothers mates

Fuckin hopi were you dresed like that your like a ned your brothers mates are just funny definatly that fat kunt mulky

this is the way forward dressing like this none of that gothy scally pish this is the fashion

I went into my house.

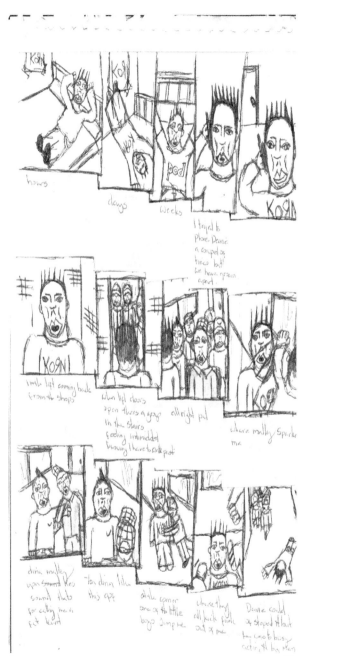

my noise burst
shot forth any I dress
not my personality

started changing
my clohs after
a couple of weeks

changing
th music
I was into

and dumping
my old clohs

mainly mornin
in school

you dressing
normal know ya
not into any of that
muslim munson
posh enjoy...

I stand out like
a sore thumb at
school started
growing apart

O you just
look like a
sceemy

I started not hanging
about with him any
more its all rich
dressing like that because
they come from a posh
area

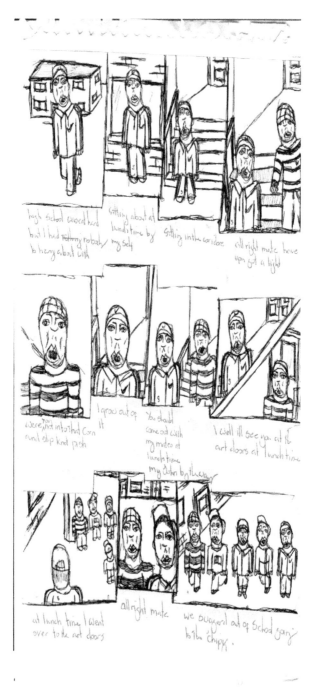

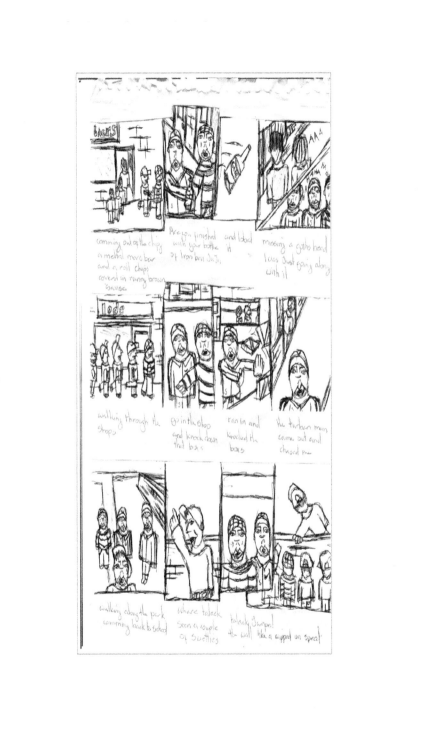

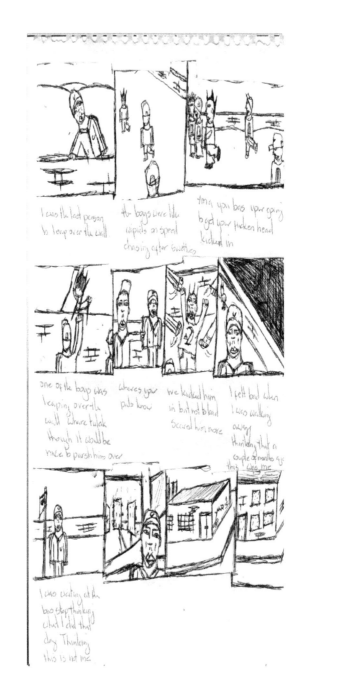

I was the last person to leap over the wall.

the boys were like culprits on speed chasing after sweeties

Ima you bas your going b get your fucken head kicked in

one of the boys was leaping over the wall where I look though it would be nice to push him over

wheres your pub krow

we kicked him in but not blind Scared him more

I felt bad when I was walking away thinking that a couple of months ago this was me

I was waiting at the bus stop thinking what I did that day Thinking this is not me

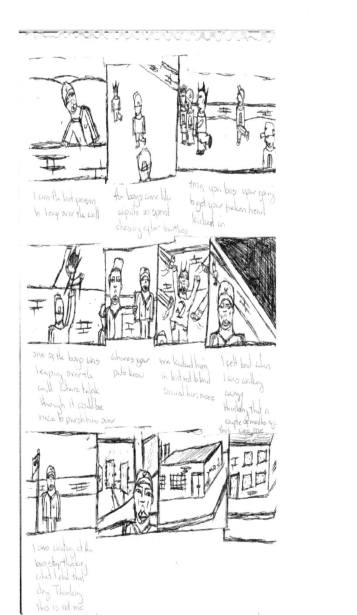

after seeing that we leged it

the door swing open Right yet wee kunts

chased us down the stairs

it was a bit like Indeanna Jones with the ball comming down.

where me a Dav swing one off stairs doors open and hid next to the bin shed

trying to catch our breath but think I was twiching cloth.

pressed the lift

outside where we meet up with the rest of the boys

where Ryan had a plan for tomorrow Saturday.

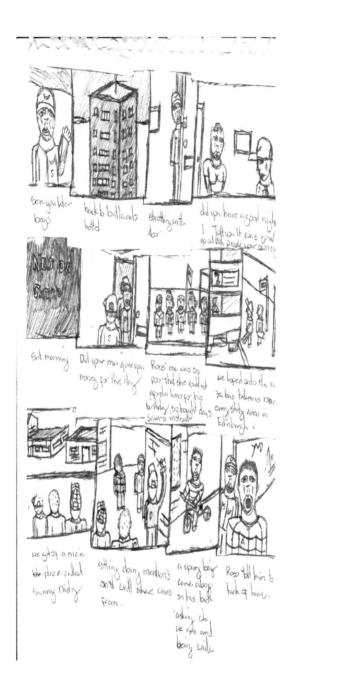

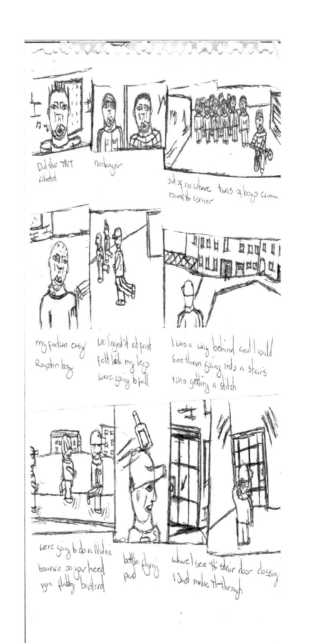

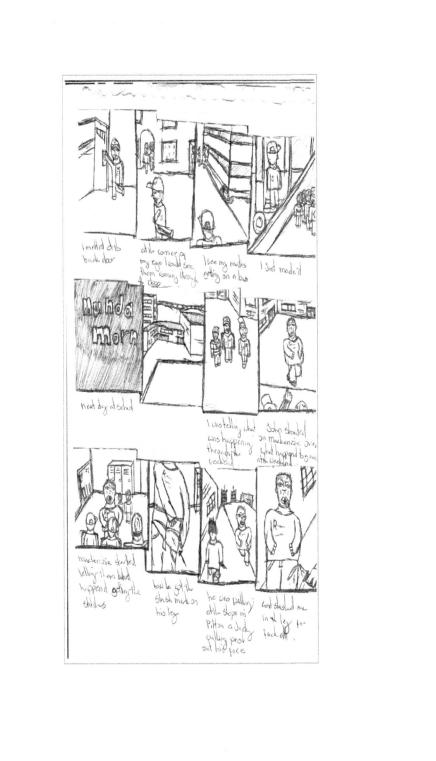

na

Ryan had a bright Idea
diging out spuds

this is what I was
looking for

why the fuck
do you have
spuds when
ryan dont have
a garden

We can dig a trentch in the wastland
so the police cant see us.

We all took turns diging
the hole

Dave at least I got m
hole this week

milky kept poping up   The riot van stoped

We were hiding but we could
here the walkie talkies gettin
luder as they were coming clos

after a while
they left

Finaly got back to the park   daing dizy
o we thought you did a runer   lizys + taking
with the money said Davie   cap abouts through the eye.

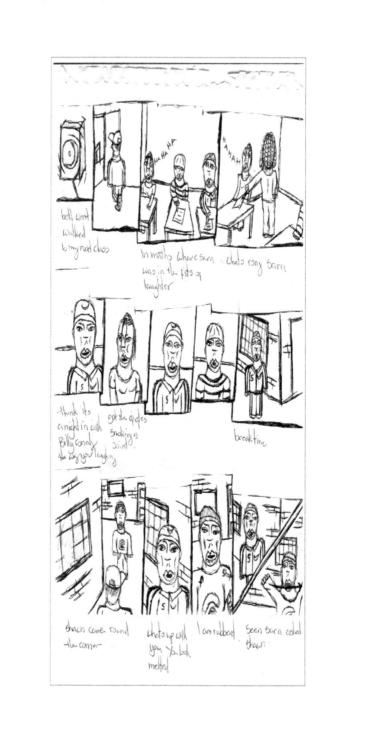

everyone outside the pub was
fighting I think it was her
cousin cars/cabs .

bin getting
pulled apart
taken as weapons

there were somens ges
in the middle of the fight

It guy gets pulled out
a pub

and gets his head
kicked about

people are pilling
at the door at the chines

Someone comes by
through the chines

the chines man comes out
screaming and shouting

people taking of the
belts and then going
teens come running

people getting bottled
gushing of blood

front row tickets to a fight   Ryan said theres the buses

bits of them came   Rosso was 1st   I was sittin in   wish something
flying out   to run   a pub lookin   would happen
                                              at penn's bird
                                              out my head

some boy came over   he bounded   shaying some   I'm off to get a cabab
steaming   like big pips   poor guys legs
                           going up an
                           down doing the
                           legs and arms
                           dance

we went to Somerfield
to look at the board
to see if there was
any cars for sale

phoning all different numbers
saying we had passed our
test

Jump in

when did you
get this

Jumped in the
back

revving it up

where do you
want to go

Shit
slow down three suits lazies

when did you
start driving

that Jumped
in were all
crammed

I'm only hoping
I don't get a
stiffy

Roskings just showing
of your things he was a
very shit driver going ran
th streets

burn it

Sara started crying
Stop Stop
what said Rasko

Mazug got out the
car

See you later
you just fucked it
up Rasko

The police went
past. The shit
was turning the
cloth

I think I skipped
a heart beat

here mallys ma.
Beped to horn

going past we
all ducked t down
as if no one was
In the car.

Just pull it
in over here
at the park

We got out

and burnt
it out got
was stollen.

Mon morning
at School

break time
coco is the hardest
person in school

are you
easy about
him
what do you
mean Am I
easy

think was
had found
a car window
open

look what
I chard

Oh here c
coco

All right

Score goals
here
look at you you dress
like a tramp boes in your dress

Then he
walked
away

were in class
where I was
thinking how
I was going
to get out of this

ya better
fight him

the bell
went for
next class into proomy

where John
seen coco.

Said I was easy for
after school

no way I got out it I h
to fight him .

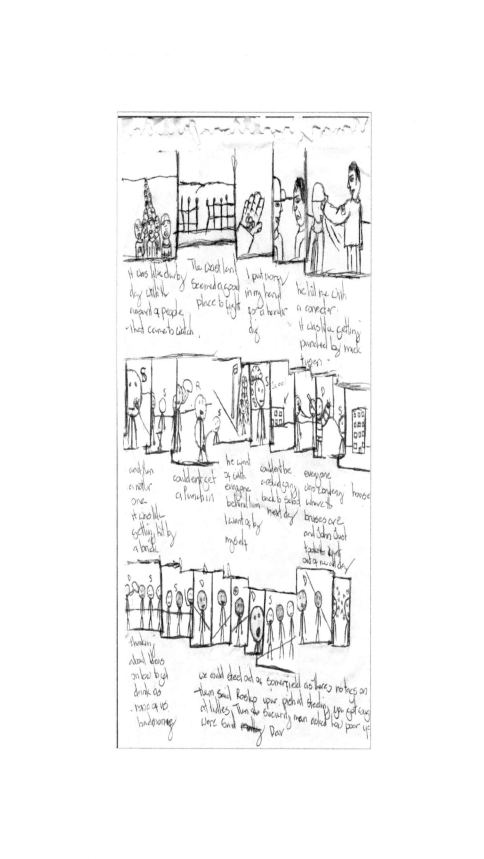

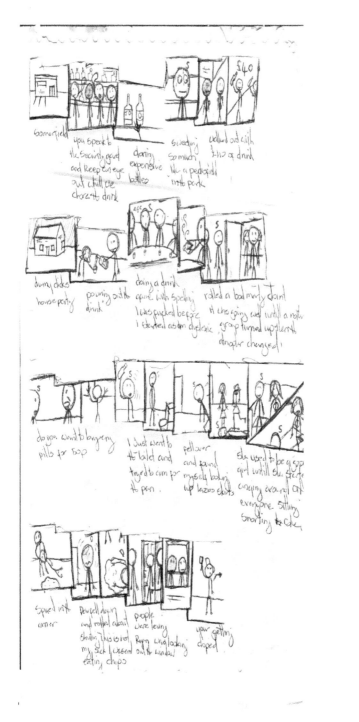

we ran out the front
when he come
round the corner
starting YMD.

Just
managed
to close the
door

ladies
were
crying

blades
coming
through
the letter
box

then they
legged it as
the police
came

next day in my
house sitting doin
home work

Went round
to Roscos 1st
time being in Roscos
house all he had was
a TV and play station in the corner

Thought you
had loaf gone
I see it got was
Shit

he had
no carpets
and nothing
in the kitchen

tone how I know
Dav and that sing
him

Ryan phoned
asking if were
going to the Shops
to hang around

hanging
about it
Shops like
not the point of
a light bulb.

here comes Daves brother
Dith Chris

Chris was going on about how
he batterd some boy last
week and singing hard
songs.

They were heading
up to a house

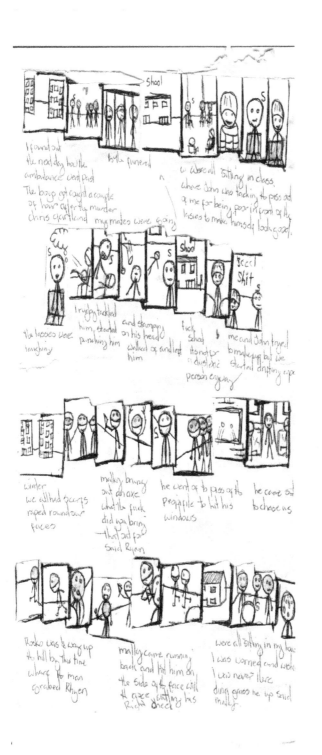

With nothing to do round the winter Peachville was to modern day with him.

Mally was running his window with stones and Ryan was mooning him.

He came flying out with a knife and chased us down the street.

Shitting ourself but loving it at the same time Ryan was struggling to pull up his trous

We hit his window and kick his door

put wheely bin against his door so when he opend it he would fall in.

We saved up money to get fire works and thought of every way to youse them. We chucked bangers at windows and put them in electric boxes.

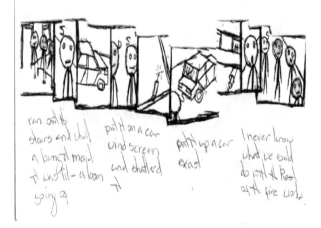

ran onto the stairs and chuck a bunch maybe it was till a loam going of

put it on a car wind screen and shattered it

put it up a car exast

I never know what we could do with the rest of the fire works.

Shan
Ada
Ryan
Muj
Diso
David
John.
Davie

YNT

With nothing to do round the winter, Reece was on to Alex and me maybe every day with him.

mostly Alex torturing his blindad with stones and Kyan was moaning him

Shitting ourselves he came flying out with a knife and chased us down the street

he came flying but loving it the same time Ky and chased us down was dancing to pull up his tra...

he hit his window and lock his door

put wheely bin against his door so when he sprang it he would fall in

we saved up money, bought fire works and thought of every way to use them we chucked bangers at windows and put them in electric boxes

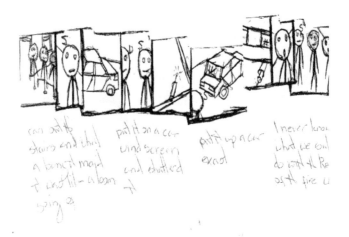

on onto the stairs and chucked a bunch maybe t and lit - a loom going on

put it in a car wind screen and chucked it

put it up a car exost

I never know what we could do with the Re as th fire u...

BOOK

THE END

you know
your life
is fucked
up when you have to take
your mates with you
when you go out to
chippy because
they acted like the
big man for so many
years but were
all talk.

What did
I do. Edinburgh is probably not
the city for me but I wrote a
book about it.

Rest in Peace the sovie ring bottle of bucky
and the burbary cap.

Kiss this

Printed in Great Britain
by Amazon

21161747R00047